BABY DRAGONS

Coloring Book

This Coloring book belongs to

COLOR TEST PAGE

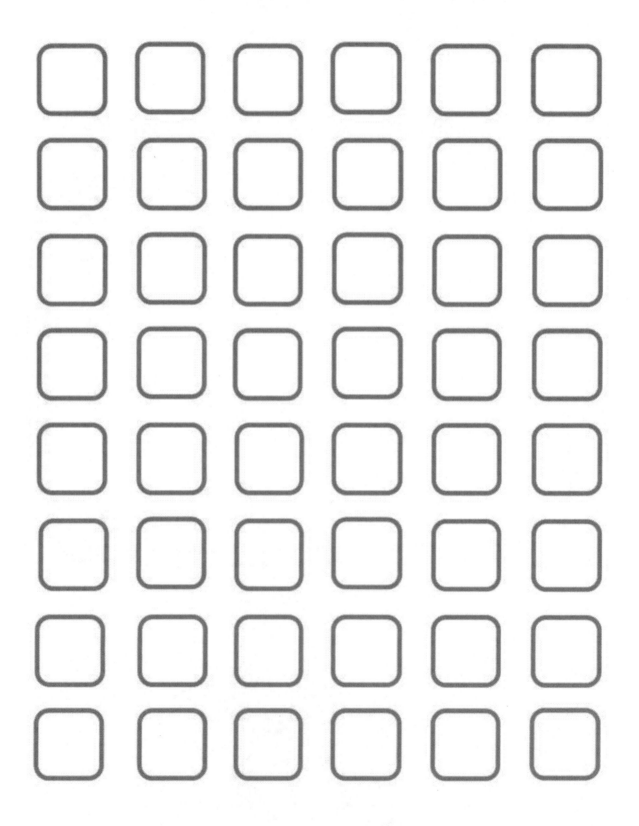

We LOVE to hear from you.
If you liked this book, please, leave us a review in Amazon. We would be very thankful.

SCAN ME

Thank you!

Made in United States
Troutdale, OR
11/15/2024

24862271R00060